THIS IS A BORZOI BOOK PUBLISHED BY ALFRED A. KNOPF

Copyright © 2001, 2003 by Hachette Livre
All rights reserved under International and Pan-American Copyright Conventions. Published in the
United States of America by Alfred A. Knopf, a division of Random House, Inc. New York, and
simultaneously in Canada by Random House of Canada Limited, Toronto. Distributed by Random House, Inc.
New York. Originally published in France as Gaspard et Lisa s'ennuient by Hachette Jeunesse in 2001.
KNOPF, BORZOI BOOKS, and the colophon are registered trademarks of Random House, Inc.
www.randomhouse.com/kids
Library of Congress Cataloging-in-Publication Data.
Gutman, Anne.
[Gaspard et Lisas ennuient. English.]
Gaspard and Lisa's rainy day / Anne Gutman, Georg Hallensleben.—1st Borzoi Books ed.
p. cm.—(Misadventures of Gaspard and Lisa)
Summary: One rainy day, two young friends search in vain for something to do that won't upset
their parents or grandmother.
ISBN 0-375-82252-6
[1. Boredom—Fiction. 2. Behavior—Fiction. 3. Friendship—Fiction.] I. Hallensleben, Georg. II. Title. III. Series.
PZ7.G9844 Gap 2003 [Fic]—dc21   2002002000
First Borzoi Books edition: March 2003 Printed in France 10 9 8 7 6 5 4 3 2 1

ANNE GUTMAN · GEORG HALLENSLEBEN

Gaspard and Lisa's Rainy Day

Alfred A. Knopf ❧ New York

Gaspard and I were on vacation
at my grandma's, and it
rained every single day.

It was too cold and muddy to play outside,
and there was nothing to do indoors!

"Let's make a cake!" said Grandma. She laid out
the ingredients, then left to get some aprons.

We couldn't wait to get started.

Gaspard made the batter and
I made the frosting. But when
Grandma returned . . .

. . . "Oh, what a mess!" she cried.

We were sent to our rooms. But I had a fun idea.
We could make a haunted house! First we had
to make a trap that would roll down the stairs
if someone stepped on it.

Then we made the room dark and scary.
"The first person who enters will
die of fright," said Gaspard.

The first person was Mom.
She got mad and told us
to play downstairs.

Downstairs, Dad was watching tennis on television. That gave me another good idea. I found two tennis rackets and we started our own game . . .

. . . in the dining room. That made Dad mad. He yelled,
"Stop it before you break something!" Then he asked,
'Why can't you put a puzzle together like other children?"

While the grown-ups were napping, we decided that Grandma's rabbit-and-pheasant poster would make a great puzzle.

We would cut it into tiny pieces, and then when we finished the puzzle, we would just tape it together and hang it up again, and no one would notice anything.

So we cut the poster ...

...into many tiny pieces,

did the puzzle,

and taped it together again. But—OH, NO!

We were missing part of the rabbit.
We looked everywhere, but we couldn't find
the missing piece.

"Don't worry," said Gaspard.
"I can fix it with my colored markers."

But none of his markers were the same color
as the rabbit. Grandma was going to be furious.

When Mom and Dad woke up,
they came to the living room.
We were very scared . . .
especially when Dad sat
right in front of our puzzle.

And then Grandma arrived.
"Look at THAT!" she said.
"Look at what?" asked Dad.
We held our breath. It was terrible.

So we all went out into the garden.

As for the puzzle, we would buy
the right colored marker.
And then no one would ever know.